Chicago and the Cat

WRITTEN AND ILLUSTRATED BY

Robin Michal Koontz

A LITTLE CHAPTER BOOK

COBBLEHILL BOOKS · DUTTON/NEW YORK

This book is for our beloved Underfoot,
who shared her mice with us for fourteen years

Grateful acknowledgment to Rosanne and Joe Ann,
who keep taking chances, and with special thanks
for my good friend Barbara Gregorich (aka Chicago):
May we both endeavor to persevere.

Library of Congress Cataloging-in-Publication Data
Koontz, Robin Michal.
Chicago and the cat / written and illustrated by
Robin Michal Koontz.   p.   cm.
Summary: A pushy cat takes over the home of
Chicago the rabbit, but then the two become friends.
ISBN 0-525-65097-0
[1. Rabbits—Fiction.   2. Cats—Fiction.
3. Friendship—Fiction.]   I. Title.
PZ7.K83574Ch   1992   [E]—dc20   91-34863   CIP   AC

Published in the United States by Cobblehill Books,
an affiliate of Dutton Children's Books,
a division of Penguin Books USA Inc.,
375 Hudson Street, New York, New York 10014

Typography by Kathleen Westray
Printed in Hong Kong   First Edition
10 9 8 7 6 5 4 3 2 1

CHAPTER ONE

The
Unexpected Guest

"Watch out!"

Chicago jumped back from the door.

"Gangway, coming through!"

The cat whizzed past Chicago.

"Who are you?" Chicago yelled.

The cat disappeared into
Chicago's kitchen.

"Come back here!"

Chicago thumped after the cat.

"What's for supper?" asked the cat.

She opened Chicago's refrigerator.

"Shut that door," Chicago said.

"All I have is lettuce, carrots,
and zucchini; no cat food."

"You must have something I like,"
said the cat.

The cat whooshed into the dining room.

She reached across the table.

"Oops!"

Chicago came running.

"My favorite cookie jar!" cried Chicago.

"My favorite cookies!" the cat exclaimed.

"Yummmm, delicious!"

"Okay, cat, it's time for you to go."

Chicago held the door open.

"Brrrr, it's cold in here," said the cat.

"Shouldn't you get some firewood?"

"That's what I was going to do
when you showed up," said Chicago.

Chicago went outside.

The cat shut the door.

Chicago knocked at the door.

"Let me in, please," she said.

"Who is it?" asked the cat.

"Let me in, you cat you!"

Chicago banged on the door.

"All right, all right," said the cat.

She opened the door.

Chicago rushed in.

"What was the big idea,

locking me outside like that?"

Chicago asked.

"I was just kidding you," said the cat.

"Can't you take a joke?"

"That was not a funny joke,"
 said Chicago.
"It's freezing and snowing outside."
"Goodness," said the cat.
"And you wanted to send me out there,
 in the freezing snow?"
"Gee," said Chicago, "I guess not."
"But tomorrow morning
 you must be on your way."

CHAPTER TWO

The Next Morning

"Chicago, wake up!" a voice yelled.
Chicago threw off the covers
and grabbed for her slippers.
"What is it? Fire? Flood? Earthquake?"
She rubbed her eyes and looked around.
The cat stood in her doorway.
"It's time for breakfast," said the cat.

"What is that terrible smell?"
asked Chicago.

"Tuna fish pancakes," said the cat.

"I borrowed a can of tuna
from your neighbor."
The cat shoved a plate of pancakes
under Chicago's nose.

"Yuk, get those away from me!"
said Chicago.

"But I made carrot pancakes for you,"
  said the cat.

"Carrot pancakes?" Chicago took
  the plate.

"I've never had carrot pancakes."

"Let's go to the dining room," said the cat.

"The rest of our breakfast is waiting."

"I hope you like fresh lettuce juice,"
said the cat.
She poured a cup for Chicago.
"How about some zucchini bread?"
She passed Chicago a basket of bread.

"Thank you," said Chicago.
Chicago took a bite of her pancakes.
She tasted the bread.

"Delicious!" she exclaimed.

Chicago gulped down the lettuce juice.

"I didn't know cats could cook!"

The cat poured Chicago another
cup of juice.

"I think you're going to like
having me around," said the cat.

CHAPTER THREE

The
Vegetable Garden

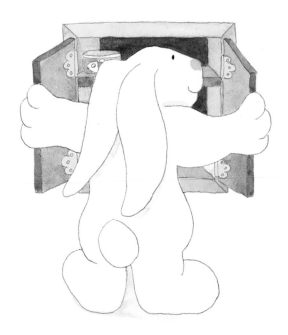

Chicago looked in the refrigerator.

"We're almost out of lettuce and

zucchini!" she exclaimed.

"Hmmmmmm," said the cat.

Chicago rummaged in the root cellar.

"We're nearly out of carrots!" she shouted.

"Really?" said the cat.

"How's the tuna fish supply?"

Chicago searched the cupboards.

"You're down to your last can," she said.

The cat jumped up.

"We need to go to the store!"

she exclaimed.

"We'll go to the store tomorrow,"

said Chicago.

"Today I must plant the vegetable garden!"

Chicago ran outside.

"Gardening sounds like hard work,"

said the cat.

"I guess I'll take a nap."

Mr. Walturs strolled into the yard.

"What are you planting?" he asked.

"Lettuce, zucchini, and carrots,"
said Chicago.

"Try some of my super-dooper
fertilizer," said Mr. Walturs.

"It'll grow super-dooper vegetables!"

"Wow, thanks," said Chicago.

She sniffed at the bottle.

"It sure smells funny," she said.

"It's fish fertilizer," said Mr. Walturs.

"Made from pure fish oil!"

"It'll grow super-dooper vegetables?"
asked Chicago.

"You bet!" said Mr. Walturs.

The next morning, Chicago went outside
to admire her garden.
The cat was sunning in Chicago's hammock.
Chicago's garden was a total mess.
"What happened to my garden?"
cried Chicago.

"It was delicious," said
the cat.
"A little gritty, but
no bones."
"You ate my garden?"
Chicago stared at
the cat in disbelief.
"Seeds, dirt, and all?"

The cat burped.

"Oh, no," she explained.

"Just the fishy stuff.

I spat out the dirt and seeds."

Chicago sighed.

"Now can we go to the store?"

asked the cat.

"We may as well," said Chicago.

CHAPTER FOUR

A
New Friend

"We should get a dog," announced Chicago.

"What for?" asked the cat.

"For a friend, a protector," said Chicago.

"But dogs eat cats!" cried the cat.

"Don't be silly," said Chicago.

"Dogs don't eat cats."

"Is that so?" replied the cat.

"What about Mr. Walturs' dog?"

"Big Jake just wants to play with you,"
said Chicago.

"Right," said the cat.

"That's why he snarls and drools
whenever he sees me."

"Okay, maybe Big Jake tries to eat cats,"
admitted Chicago.

"But we won't get a dog like Big Jake."

Chicago and the cat arrived
at the animal shelter.
They looked in the cages.
"This puppy is cute," said Chicago.
"Yip! Yip! Yip!" said the puppy.
"They're noisy!" cried the cat.
She held her ears.
"They smell yucky, too!"
She held her nose.

"May I help you?"
asked the shelter volunteer.

"We want a canary," said the cat.

"No, we don't," said Chicago.

"We would like to adopt a dog.

One that doesn't try to eat cats."

"And doesn't bark or smell yucky,"

added the cat.

"Fred here needs a good home,"

said the volunteer.

She held up a tattered toy dog.

"Fred has been warming puppies

for many years,

and now he's ready to retire."

"He's perfect!" exclaimed the cat.

"We won't even have to feed him!"

Chicago looked at Fred.

"I don't know," she said.

"What kind of a protector will he be?"

"What kind of a friend?"

"We'll set him in the window

to protect us," said the cat.

"And you already have me for a friend!"

Chicago and the cat headed home.

"It'll be fun having a dog after all,"

said the cat.

"Right," said Chicago.